# Riddledy Piggledy

*I'm Mother Goose. Come, take a look.*
*I've put together a riddle book.*
*Read out each rhyme and guess the song*
*where all the riddledy things belong.*

# Riddledy Piggledy

## Tony Mitton

*Illustrated by*
Paddy Mounter

**d|b** FICKLING

David Fickling Books

OXFORD · NEW YORK

A DAVID FICKLING BOOK

Published by David Fickling Books
an imprint of Random House Children's Books
a division of Random House, Inc.
New York

Published simultaneously in Canada by Random House of Canada Limited, Toronto.
Originally published in Great Britain by David Fickling Books, an imprint of
Random House Children's Books.

www.randomhouse.com/kids

Library of Congress Cataloging-in-Publication Data is available upon request.
ISBN 0-385-75024-2 (trade)
ISBN 0-385-75033-1 (lib. bdg.)

MANUFACTURED IN MALAYSIA

September 2004
10 9 8 7 6 5 4 3 2 1
First American Edition

# Contents

*To Mum, with love.*
TM *x*

# Soggy Boggy Bag

A doctor's bag
in a bit of a muddle
dropped beside a very deep puddle,
lost in Gloucester in a shower of rain
(but nobody came back
to get it again).

What's the answer? Let me see · · ·
Have a think. Now, what can it be · · ·?

# Picnic Website

A bowl and a spoon
(with cobwebs on),
but nobody knows
where the owner's gone.

What's the answer? Let me see · · ·
Have a think. Now, what can it be · · ?

# Little Miss Muffet

Little Miss Muffet
sat on a tuffet,
eating her curds and whey.
Along came a spider
who sat down beside her
and frightened
Miss Muffet away.

# Table for Two

A table for two with the diners gone,
and none of the dishes have anything on.
Maybe they were hungry,
or greedy, or neat,
as they've just left dishes,
but nothing to eat.

*What's the answer? Let me see . . .*
*Have a think. Now, what can it be . . . ?*

# Jack Sprat

Jack Sprat could eat no fat.
His wife could eat no lean.
And so between the two of them,
they licked the platter clean.

# Peepo! Sheep-Ho!

A flock of sheep,
and they're on the roam.
Maybe they'll find
their own way home . . . ?

What's the answer? Let me see · · ·
Have a think. Now, what can it be · · ?

# Little Bo-Peep

Little Bo-Peep has lost her sheep
and doesn't know where to find them.
Leave them alone, and they will come home,
bringing their tails behind them.

# Beep-Beep!
# Boy Asleep!

Here by a haystack,
not far from the corn,
someone's been sleeping –
they've dropped their horn.

*What's the answer? Let me see . . .
Have a think. Now, what can it be . . . ?*